Weekly Reader Children's Book Club
presents

THORNTON
THE WORRIER

by Marjorie Weinman Sharmat

illustrated by Kay Chorao

Holiday House • New York

This book is a presentation of Weekly
Reader Children's Book Club.
Weekly Reader Children's Book Club
offers book clubs for children from
preschool to young adulthood. All
quality hardcover books are selected
by a distinguished Weekly Reader
Selection Board.

For further information write to:
Weekly Reader Children's Book Club
1250 Fairwood Ave.
Columbus, Ohio 43216

Library of Congress Cataloging in Publication Data

Sharmat, Marjorie Weinman.
Thornton, the worrier.

SUMMARY: Thornton Rabbit worries about everything until he meets an old man who worries about
nothing.
[1. Worry—Fiction]   I.   Chorao, Kay.
II. Title.
PZ7.S5299Th   [E]   78-1286
ISBN 0-8234-0328-9

For my mother,
who said "Be joyful."

All the animals in the neighborhood were busy.

"I am learning new card tricks," said Daisy Beaver.

"I am sewing a new suit," said Basil Hippopotamus.

"I am writing an opera," said Lynden Muskrat.

"I am worrying," said Thornton Rabbit.

"Worrying?" said Basil. "That is no way to keep busy."

"It keeps me very busy," said Thornton. "All day and into the night, I worry. I don't even have time to watch my favorite program on television."

"What are you worried about?" asked Daisy.

"Well," said Thornton, "I am worried about toothaches, bad weather, my house falling down, mosquito bites, hunger, enemies, and assorted disasters."

"I never thought there were so many things to worry about," said Daisy.

"Yes. I am even worried because there are so many things to worry about," said Thornton. "The minute I am finished with one, I get a new one."

"I can see that it does keep you busy," said Basil.

"It certainly does," said Thornton.

Time passed. Daisy learned card tricks. Lynden wrote. Basil sewed. And Thornton worried.

"What are you worried about today?" Basil asked Thornton.

"I am worried about today," said Thornton.

"Why don't you try to cheer up?" said Daisy. "Look in the mirror and tell yourself, 'Everything is okay. I am okay. Today is okay. Tomorrow will be okay.'"

"I will try that," said Thornton.

He went into his house and looked in the mirror. He said, "Everything is okay. I am okay. Today is okay. Tomorrow will be okay. I am funny looking."

Thornton went outside.

"I looked in the mirror," he said, "and I found out that I am more funny looking than I was yesterday. I am growing funnier looking every day. Now what should I do?"

"I don't know," said Lynden.
"I give up," said Daisy.
"So do I," said Basil.
Thornton walked away.

"Pretty soon I won't have any friends," he thought.

Thornton walked on. "I am a funny looking rabbit who is losing his friends and whose house might fall down and who might get fleas and die or maybe get very sick and not die at all but just get funnier looking every day."

Thornton sat down. "I am a mess," he said.

Thornton sat and worried. Then he got up and walked and worried until he came to a path. The path went up and up. Thornton went up and up. At last he came to a house.

Thornton stopped and rubbed his eyes. "This house is sitting on the edge of a mountain! Half of it is on and half of it is off. This house will fall down!"

Thornton knocked on the door of the house. An old man opened the door.

"Your house will fall over!" said Thornton.

"I'm happy to meet you, too," said the man.

"Your house will fall over!" said Thornton again.

"Come in," said the man, "and have something to eat."

"Aren't you worried that your house will fall over?" asked Thornton.

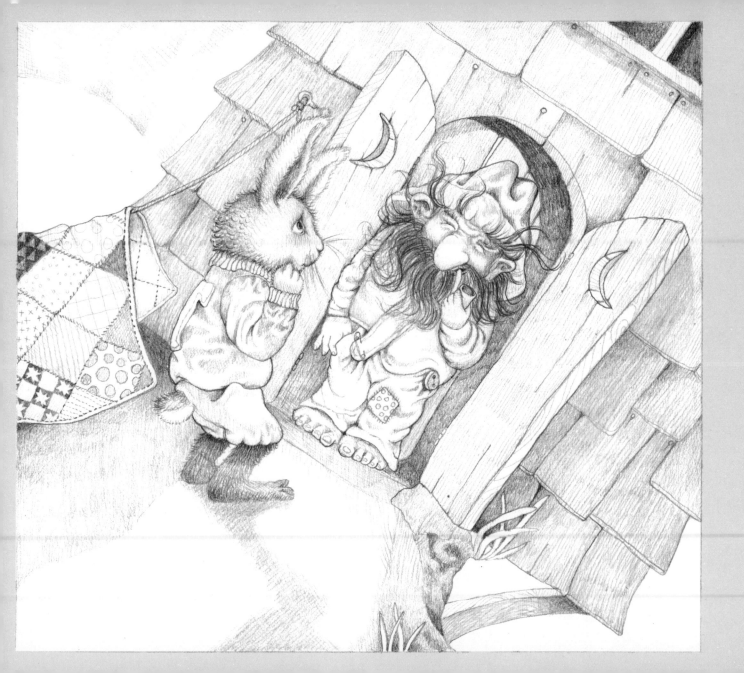

"I never worry," said the man.

"But your house is half on land and half on air," said Thornton.

"Yes, I know," said the man. "It has always been that way. But I don't think about it. This is a happy house and I am happy in it. I read my newspapers, paint my furniture, mend my clothes, eat breakfast, lunch, dinner, and snacks, and I dream a lot."

Roomumph!

"What's that?" asked Thornton.

"That's a leaning noise," said the man. "Every now and then my house leans over a bit more."

"Horrors!" said Thornton.

OROOOMUMPH! OROOOMUMPH!

"It's getting worse," said Thornton. "I am so worried I can't stand it."

"Nothing to worry about," said the man.

OHRUMMPAH MUUMPH ROOOUMPH WHOOSH!

"*I'm really worried!*" cried Thornton, as the house started to fall down the mountain.

Thornton grabbed the man and pulled him out of the house.

"Whew, thanks!" said the man. "You know, maybe I should have worried a little."

"But if you had worried," said Thornton, "you would not have enjoyed your house all the years you lived in it. You would not have enjoyed all the breakfasts and lunches and dinners and snacks and dreaming and reading your newspapers and mending your clothes and painting your furniture. You would not have enjoyed any of those things."

"I know," said the man.

"Are you worried that you don't have a house anymore?" asked Thornton.

"No," said the man. "I will find another one."

Thornton said goodbye to the man and started home.

"That man has nothing to worry about. And I have everything to worry about. How can that be?"

Thornton looked up. "Perhaps I do not have to worry about everything. There is a mosquito up there, and maybe he is going to bite me and maybe he isn't. You don't worry me, Mosquito! If you bite me, I'll bite you back!"

Thornton walked on. Then he bent down and looked in a stream.

"I see my face in there. It looks wiggly and wavy but it does not look funny looking. My face must be happy. I do not have to worry about my face."

Thornton looked around. "Today is a nice day," he said. "It is pretty. The air smells sweet. Today is doing fine. I do not have to worry about today."

Thornton started to skip. "I feel good," he said.

Thornton saw Lynden and Basil and Daisy. He danced around them.

Basil stopped sewing. "Thornton never did that before," he said. "I'm worried."

Lynden stopped writing. "I'm worried, too," he said.

Daisy dropped her cards. "So am I," she said.

Thornton shouted, "I'm not worried! I'm not worried about anything!"

And he told Basil and Lynden and Daisy all about the old man and the house.

"Where will the man sleep tonight?" asked Daisy.

"Under the stars," said Thornton.

"I hope he has a warm blanket," said Lynden.

"And hot chocolate," said Basil.

"And mittens," said Daisy.

"Oh, dear," said Thornton, and he ran off.

Thornton was gone a long time. When he came back, the old man was with him.

"How do you do?" said Basil and Lynden and Daisy.

"I'm happy to meet you, too," said the old man.

Then Thornton and Basil and Daisy and Lynden helped the old man build a new house on the flattest land in the forest.

And Thornton had nothing more to worry about.